BIBLICAL VALUES FOR KIDS

LEARN TO READ

JONATHAN

SAYS

"I Can Hardly Wait!"

by Crystal Bowman
illustrated by Karen Maizel

ZondervanPublishingHouse
Grand Rapids, Michigan

A Division of HarperCollins*Publishers*

Jonathan James Says, "I Can Hardly Wait!"
Text copyright © 1997 by Crystal Bowman
Illustrations copyright © 1997 by Karen Maizel

Requests for information should be addressed to:
Zondervan Publishing House
Grand Rapids, Michigan 49530

▲ **Library of Congress Cataloging-in-Publication Data**

Bowman, Crystal.
    Jonathan James says, "I can hardly wait!" / written by
Crystal Bowman: illustrated by Karen Maizel.
      p.   cm. — (Jonathan James)
    Summary: A young rabbit learns the value of patience as
he waits for spring so he can use his new roller blades, tries
to earn money for the watch he wants, and looks forward to
Grandpa's visit.
    ISBN 0-310-21207-3
    [1. Rabbits—Fiction. 2. Patience—Fiction. 3. Christian
life—Fiction.]   I. Maizel, Karen, ill. II. Title. III. Series:
Bowman, Crystal. Jonathan James.
PZ7.B6834oj   1997
[E]—dc20   96042264
                                             CIP

Printed in the United States of America

97 98 99 00 01 /❖ DP / 10 9 8 7 6 5 4 3 2 1

For Bob,
my number-one fan

—C. B.

For Grandma Augusta,
who could hardly wait

—K. M.

CONTENTS

ROLLER BLADES

Father came home from work.

He was carrying a box.

"What's in the box?"

asked Jonathan James.

"Something for you,"
Father answered.
Jonathan opened the box.
"Oh, boy! Roller blades!" he said.
"They were on sale," said Father.
Jonathan tried them on.

"May I roller blade now?" he asked.

"Don't be silly, J.J.," said Mother.

"There is snow outside.

You will have to wait for spring."

"I will roller blade in the house,"
said Jonathan.

"Oh, no," said Mother.

"Roller blades are for outdoors."

Jonathan took off his roller blades.
But he did not want to wait
for spring.

Jonathan went to his bedroom
and closed the door.

He put on his roller blades.
He held onto his bed
so he wouldn't fall,
and he pushed himself
back and forth.
"This is fun!" Jonathan said.

Jonathan let go of his bed.

Ouch!

He bumped his head on the dresser.

His piggy bank fell
and smashed into pieces.

Mother and Father heard the noise.
"Jonathan James!" scolded Mother.
"I told you not to roller blade
in the house!"
"I'm sorry," Jonathan answered.
"We will put the roller blades
away for now," said Father.

Mother got some ice
for Jonathan's head.
"You will have to wait for spring,"
Mother said again.

Every day Jonathan
looked out the window.
Every day there was snow
on the ground.
"Spring will never come,"
sighed Jonathan.

One day,
Jonathan looked out the window,
and the sun was shining.
The birds were singing.
The snow was almost gone.

"Spring is almost here,"
said Mother.

"When may I roller blade?"
asked Jonathan.

"How about this afternoon?"
Mother replied.

"Oh, boy!" cried Jonathan.

"I can hardly wait!"

After lunch,
Jonathan put on his roller blades.
He put on his helmet and pads.
Then he skated up and down
the sidewalk.
He didn't hold on to anything.
He didn't bump his head.

And this time, he didn't even fall.

THE WATCH

It was eight o'clock in the morning.
Jonathan was eating
a bowl of cereal.
"Look," said Jonathan.
He showed Mother the cereal box.
"May I order this watch?
It glows in the dark."

Mother looked at the cereal box.

"Hmm," she said.

"It costs six dollars."

"May I get it?" Jonathan
asked again.

"You may order the watch,"
Mother told him.
"But first you must earn
the money."
"How?" asked Jonathan.
"I will pay you one dollar
an hour," said Mother.
"You will have to work
for six hours."

"What can I do?" he asked.

"First you can sweep the steps," she said.

"Then you can clean the fish bowl."

Jonathan looked at the clock.

It was nine o'clock.

Jonathan swept the steps.

Then he cleaned the fish bowl.

"There," said Jonathan, "I'm done."

But it was only ten o'clock.

"Now what can I do?" he asked.

"You can help Kelly
clean her room,"
Mother told him.

"Then you can fold that
pile of socks."

"All right," said Jonathan.

Jonathan helped Kelly
clean her room.

Then he folded all the socks.

It was eleven o'clock.

"I've only earned two dollars,"
Jonathan complained.

"You can earn more money
tomorrow," said Mother.

The next day,
Jonathan helped Father
rake leaves.
It took a long time,
but he earned two more dollars.

Jonathan bagged leaves
the next day.
Then he counted his dollar bills.
One, two, three, four, five, six.
"Now I can order my watch!"
said Jonathan.
"Yes, you can," said Mother.
"We are proud of you," said Father.

Jonathan ordered his watch.

Every day he checked the mailbox.

Jonathan could hardly wait

for his watch to come.

"It's here!" cried Jonathan one day.

Jonathan wore his watch all day.

Jonathan wore his watch all night.
And it really did glow in the dark.

WAITING FOR THANKSGIVING

Mother was reading a letter.

"It is from Grandpa," she said.

"He is coming for Thanksgiving."

"Oh, boy!" cried Jonathan.

"Is today Thanksgiving?"

"No," said Mother.

"Today is not Thanksgiving.

You will just have to wait."

Jonathan went to his bedroom.

"Dear God," he prayed,

"thank you for my bed.

Thank you for my bear.

Thank you for my roller blades.

Thank you for my watch. Amen.

Now it is Thanksgiving
because I am thankful,"
Jonathan told Mother.
"I am happy you are thankful,"
said Mother.
"But it is not Thanksgiving."

Jonathan was sad.

He wanted it to be Thanksgiving.

He wanted Grandpa to come.

Jonathan found his crayons
and paper.

He drew a picture of a turkey.

"See the turkey?"

Jonathan asked Mother.

"Now it is Thanksgiving."

"That is a nice turkey," said Mother.
"But it is not Thanksgiving yet."

Jonathan was sad.

He wanted it to be Thanksgiving.

He wanted Grandpa to come.

The next day,

Mother was busy in the kitchen.

First she cleaned the turkey.

Then she peeled potatoes.

Then she made a pumpkin pie.

"Is today Thanksgiving?"
asked Jonathan.

"No," answered Mother.

"Today is not Thanksgiving.
But it will be Thanksgiving
tomorrow."

"Good," said Jonathan.

"I can hardly wait."

The next morning,
Jonathan heard a
knock-knock-knock.
"It's Grandpa!" he shouted.

Jonathan gave Grandpa a big hug.
"Happy Thanksgiving, J.J.,"
Grandpa said.
"Happy Thanksgiving,"
Jonathan answered.

Jonathan and his family
went to church.
Then they sat down to eat
a big Thanksgiving dinner.
"Dear Lord," Father prayed,
"we thank you for our food."
"And for Grandpa!"
Jonathan added.
"Amen!" everyone said together.

Then Jonathan ate turkey, corn,
and potatoes.
And for dessert, he had a big piece
of pumpkin pie.

Make Jonathan James your friend!

Jonathan James Says, "I Can Be Brave!"

Jonathan James is afraid. His new bedroom is too dark. He's going into first grade. And he has to stay at Grandma's overnight for the first time. What should he do? These lively, humorous stories will show new readers that sometimes things that seem scary can actually be fun!

ISBN: 0-310-49591-1

Jonathan James Says, "Let's Be Friends!"

Jonathan James is making new friends. In four easy-to-read stories, Jonathan meets a missionary, a physically challenged boy, and a new neighbor. New readers will learn important lessons about friendship and that friends like us just for who we are.

ISBN: 0-310-49601-2

Jonathan James Says, "I Can Help!"

Jonathan James is growing up, and that means he can help! In four stories written especially for new readers, Jonathan learns to pitch in and help his family—sometimes successfully and sometimes not. Young readers will learn that they can help, too!

ISBN: 0-310-49611-X

Jonathan James Says, "Let's Play Ball!"

Jonathan wants to learn how to play baseball. But who will teach him? Will he ever actually hit the ball? Fun-filled stories will teach young readers that, with practice, they can succeed in whatever they try.

ISBN: 0-310-49621-7

Jonathan James Says, "School's Out!"

Hurrah! Jonathan James makes it through the last day of school and gets to spend the summer fishing with his father. He even goes on a trip to Bible camp! In short stories that new readers will love, Jonathan learns how to be flexible … and your young reader can too!

ISBN: 0-310-21209-X

Jonathan James Says, "I Can Hardly Wait!"

Waiting is hard, especially for Jonathan James! When Jonathan receives new roller blades from his dad during the winter, can he wait until spring before trying them out? Beginning readers will enjoy three humorous stories—and they'll learn about patience along the way!

ISBN: 0-310-21207-3

ZondervanPublishingHouse
Grand Rapids, Michigan 49530
http://www.zondervan.com

Crystal Bowman enjoys sharing her poems and stories with children in many different schools. "Children are so much fun," she says. "And they give me great ideas!" Crystal lives in Grand Rapids, Michigan, with her husband and three children.

Karen Maizel knew even as a child that she would be an artist one day. "God gave me clues," she says. "What do you really like to do? God may be giving you clues about the work he has for you." Karen lives near Cleveland, Ohio, with her husband and three children.

Crystal and Karen would love to hear from you. You may write them at:

Author Relations
Zondervan Publishing House
5300 Patterson Ave., S.E.
Grand Rapids, MI 49530